PETRA

PETRA

MARIANNA COPPO

 Thames & Hudson

Nothing can move me.

Not the wind.

Not time.

I don't go anywhere.

Everyone else comes to me.

I am strong.

I'm a fearsome, fearless,
mighty, magnificent mountain!

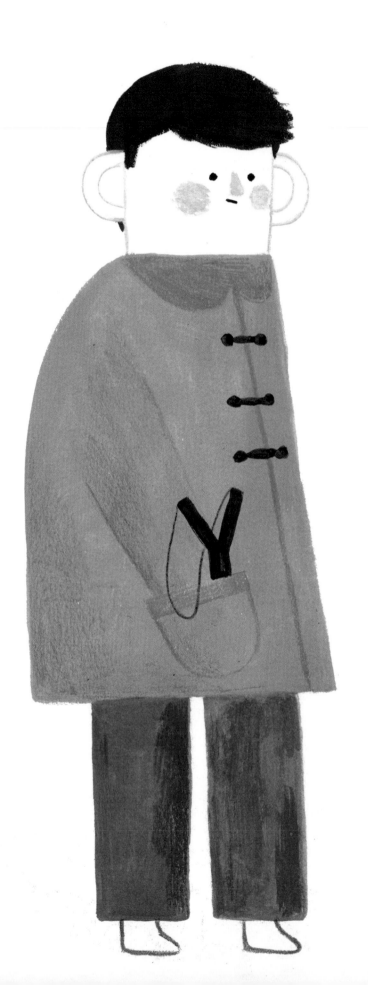

"Is that a pebble?"

"Woof!"

Me? A pebble?

No way.

I'm an egg.

A smooth and shiny egg.

An egg of the world
in a world full of surprises.

Will I breathe fire?

Will I wear a tuxedo?

Whatever I become,
I'm bound to be amazing!

"There's no room for rocks in my nest!"

Oh no, not again.

This is becoming a habit.

Well, they say no egg is an island.

But what an island!

What paradise!

What palm trees, what peace,
what sunshine, what...

-

"What a cool rock!"

Hmm, not bad at all.

What will I be tomorrow?

Who knows?

But no need to worry.

I'm a rock and this is how I roll.

Translated from the Italian *Petra*

First published in the United Kingdom in 2017 by
Thames & Hudson Ltd, 181A High Holborn, London WC1V 7QX

This paperback edition first published in 2018

Petra © 2017 Marianna Coppo
First published in Italy by Edizioni Lapis in 2016
This edition © 2017 Thames & Hudson Ltd, London
Published by arrangement with Debbie Bibo Agency

British Library Cataloguing-in-Publication Data
A catalogue record for this book is available from the British Library

ISBN 978-0-500-65178-0

Printed in China

To find out about all our publications, please visit **www.thamesandhudson.com**.
There you can subscribe to our e-newsletter, browse or download
our current catalogue, and buy any titles that are in print.